THE
Norman
Rockwell
STORYBOOK

TOLD BY JAN WAHL

Simon and Schuster
New York

Published by Simon and Schuster
A Division of Gulf & Western Corporation
Simon & Schuster Building
Rockefeller Center
1230 Avenue of the Americas
New York, New York 10020
Manufactured in the United States of America

1 2 3 4 5 6 7 8 9 10

Library of Congress Cataloging in Publication Data

Wahl, Jan.
The Norman Rockwell, storybook.

SUMMARY: Twenty, one-page, humorous stories
illustrated with paintings by Norman Rockwell.
[1. Humorous stories] I. Rockwell, Norman,
1894-1978. II. Title.
PZ7.W1266No   1979   [Fic]   79-14462

ISBN 0-671-25102-3

Norman Rockwell

BESSIE-BETWEEN

Bessie Plummer's father was Mr. Plummer the railroad man, so she knew a lot about faraway places. After all she had been out to Reno, Nevada, and as far east as Harrisburg, Pennsylvania, riding free on her father's cardboard railroad pass every summer with her mother. Maybe it was the faraway, dreamy, knowing look in her blue, blue eyes, yet both Vernon Rozinski and Willie Stackpole practically fell out of their seats whenever she glanced in their direction at school, and she had the shortest pencils of anybody because Vernon and Will were always skipping off down the aisle in hot pursuit of sharpening them.

Now Vernon and Will were close friends, at least they were in other matters. Therefore Bessie became Bessie-Between. If Vernon carried her books then Will would pick flowers for her; and Bessie just walked home, smack in the middle, thinking about some of those beautiful exciting places she'd ridden through on the railroad last summer...till one afternoon Vernon couldn't stand it anymore.

"Bessie, you'll just have to choose. Go ahead and get it done with!" he demanded.

Both Will and he stood with lumps in their throats, for their life and death depended upon what she said now.

"The Lackawanna Railroad! Oh, the Lackawanna's best," sighed Bessie in appreciation, finally—"them parlor cars with the drapes and the carpet clear over to the wall...!"

BATTER UP

The South End baseball players, popularly known as the Orang-Utang All Stars, which included among others Skinny Longnecker, the world's worst athlete, Chimp Gluss, Jr., Babe Minick, and Noodle Hennessey, also Eddie McNutt, the local runt, were having a hard time choosing up sides. They were all so bad nobody wanted anybody else on their side. Baseball being a game that is not as easy as it looks.

Well, after two hours of saying who was bad at what and worse at what else, flipping coins, matching fingers, and drawing straws, the teams finally were chosen.

Then came the question of which team would get their firsts and which would get their lasts. This was finally decided by Chimp Gluss, Jr. and Babe Minick, fist over fist on a baseball bat.

Babe Minick's team got their firsts but it took two more hours to get the batting order straight.

Chimp Gluss, Jr.'s team took the field. Skinny Longnecker stepped up to the plate. Noodle Hennessey, who was pitcher, hitched up his pants and tugged at his cap. Then he couldn't find the baseball, which after a twenty-five-minute search was located in his back pocket. And he took a long windup.

Then WHOOOOOOOOOOOOOOOOOOOO!

The five-o'clock whistle sounded from Miller's Tannery.

Game called on account of dinner!

HOME REMEDIES

Pa Fruth was out tree chopping, for his wife had been complaining the oak by the north window took up the light and she couldn't see to thread her needle. He had only gotten about two inches into the tree when he sneezed the first sneeze.

"Who's sneezing out there?" Ma called.

"Same one who's chopping so you can thread your needle!" he replied.

Well, he caught a bad cold and she brought him inside, tugging him by the ear.

"Since it's my fault you got sick—I'm going to cure you!" Ma decided then and there.

So she got Pa undressed, wrapped him up in a warm blanket, rubbed his chest with linseed oil, goosegreased his back, got out the hot water bottle, gave him dime store aspirin, nosedrops every two hours, eardrops every three hours, sulphur and molasses twice a day, sprayed his throat, put him on a liquid diet, brewed him 24-herb tea, made him sniff pine needles and garlic, gave him vitamin pills, iron deficiency extract, castor oil, plus I don't know what else, and a tub of hot water to soak his feet in.

"I'll cure you," said Ma.

"Or kill me," said Pa.

And suddenly Pa got well.

Or just sick of Ma's home remedies.

OZZIE'S TEST

All last spring Ozzie Ebersole was following Addie Clinghagen, whose family just bought a place near here. He seemed to wander about as in a daze, two steps behind her, while she dawdled the long way home to test the strength of his devotion. Up and down hills, twice through the graveyard and back.

Ozzie followed Addie, and Ozzie's dog, Scoopy, followed him. Altogether the three formed quite a parade. Ozzie didn't seem to mind, and this state of affairs went on a couple of weeks till Addie one afternoon stopped short and whirled around saying:

"Listen, mister! What are you following me for?"

Ozzie replied, clearing his throat, "Because I am interested in, um, learning if you enjoy butter!" Addie squeaked, astonished, "<u>What?</u>" so Ozzie repeated his answer.

"Why do you want to know if I enjoy butter?" she asked, smiling, growing interested and leaning closer.

"Oh, I like to know certain things about some people!" he said nervously, wishing he hadn't started the whole thing.

She kept looking at him and he had to say something so he said, "There's a good test for finding out." Addie wanted to know what that test was. So he showed her, holding a yellow flower under her chin. Ozzie gulped.

"Are you going to kiss me now?" Addie asked, puckering up.

"Right in front of Scoopy?" asked Ozzie.

The course of True Love never did run smooth. Shakespeare knows.

THE LAST FLY

Whatever Phineas Tibbs does, he likes to do it best. One thing he decided was he wouldn't waste Saturdays. And he got this excellent job at Horn's Grocery and that pretty much used up Saturday. With pocket money besides.

About the second week he was there—it was already hot, sort of a sleepy, dull, sluggish afternoon—after they had been rolling a couple barrels of Snowflake 100 Per Cent Flour into the storage room, and plagued by buzzing flies every step of the way, Mr. Horn announced, turning to him, "Phineas, you can win a dollar extra if you get rid of the <u>last one</u> of these flies. Are you the man for it?" Phineas replied he was! And Mr. Horn toddled off to find some fresh air and a calm comfortable seat, and Phineas realized he had a thousand flies to beat.

They gave him a stiff fight. But his aim was accurate and his arm quick, and within about two hours he had exterminated nearly the whole lot of them, even the ones keeping close to Mr. Horn. Word must have gotten through to the fly world that the grocery was a dangerous spot. The ranks were thinning out. Phineas was alert, in pursuit of the dozen or so remaining.

At last two flies were left. One hovered near the pickle display. Zap! He got it! The other remained atop Mr. Horn's head. Phineas dashed for it, but the grocer woke up startled, yawned, and the fly flew straight into his mouth and the poor man swallowed it. "Mr. Horn, <u>you</u> are the winner," said Phineas.

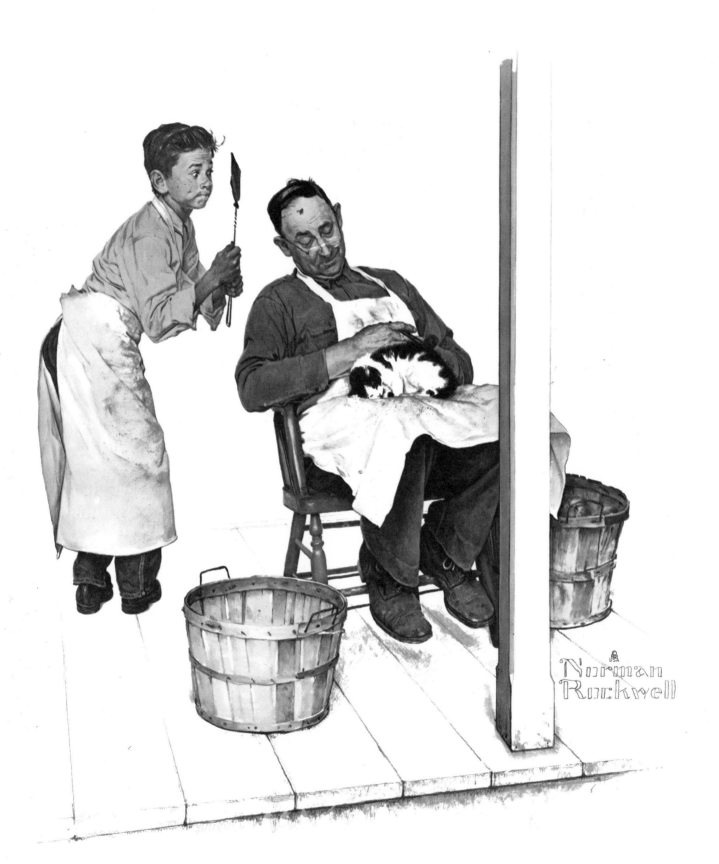

THE DREAMER

Marcus T. Jones was considered a poet and a dreamer because he spent all his time watching trains go by and folks said, Aha, he will never get ahead that way, no sir. When the whistle of the 3:47 was heard Marcus was already there waiting, half of his chores finished. He would watch it cut smartly through the hills, and he'd study it with a funny look in his eyes.

Marcus knew a lot about trains. He could tell you who invented the flat-footed T-rail. The bridge rail. The bull-headed rail. He could tell you the time of the first transcontinental run. He knew the runs of the D,T&I, the B&O, plus the C,B&Q. He knew what those letters stand for. He would go down to the Train Station and fall into a trance in front of the painted sign which said:

THIS RAILROAD STATION IS OPEN 6 A.M. TO 6 P.M.
PLEASE BUY TICKETS BEFORE BOARDING TRAIN.

then watch the activity around the station and find an open field and glance upward and maybe see a hawk circling in the sky.

He would wave to the engineers as the trains sailed off into the horizon and there were those who declared Marcus did not have his shoes planted on the ground.

Well, he is a dreamer. But not a poet. And he is going to get ahead. He is dreaming up a scheme. How to take over the railroads of America in a gigantic merger, with himself as president!

SPORTS

Skinny Longnecker one summer became the world's worst athlete. His feet and hands just didn't work together, yet he loved playing and wouldn't give up. When he'd play baseball he'd drop easy fly balls. When he'd kick a football he'd kick a teammate instead. And he couldn't sink a basket for love or money. Word spread around that Skinny was growing discouraged.

One afternoon, Skinny's mother was hanging clothes out in the back yard and he just stood there moping around. "I'm going to quit sports forever!" he announced with a sour face, loud enough so that the gang, Babe, Birdie, and Chimp, watching on the other side of the fence could hear.

The gang instantly held a meeting and decided they would rather change the rules than lose Skinny. Henceforward, striking out would get you on base. Kicking a teammate was worth two points. Missing a basket was four points. And not sinking a putt was as good as a hole-in-one. They scrambled over the back-yard fence to tell him the news.

"Okay, I'll try again," he moaned, and got out the golf clubs and stuck a tin coffee can in the ground for a hole and tied a kerchief to a beanpole and stuck it in the hole and gave his leg a wiggle and his putter a twitch and stroked the ball towards the hole—and he missed!

Everybody congratulated him on his performance!

It's not just that Skinny has a good personality. His dad owns the Sporting Goods Store.

SEA SERPENT

Ask Grandpa Penny about it and he will tell you. He claims to have a photo of it stuck in some drawer. Lizzie Kissell the church organist was the first to have spotted it swimming along calmly as you please. Believe me, says Grandpa, she hollered. Word got into town quick and the newly elected sheriff and his men drove up in their Ford, but whatever it was had fled. Then Reverend Hepplewhite of the Ridge Church saw it himself. Just a fleeting glimpse. Some claimed it was long and dull-looking; some said it was short and full of colors as the rainbow; a lot of people, anyway, found excuses to meander down by the river, and Hinkle's Hardware Store had a special going on, on binoculars, for a couple weeks.

It was dust on the surface of the river, claimed some. It was a rubber raft, claimed others. It was a thirty-foot trout that had swum from far away, said somebody else. The only thing everybody was agreed on was there was something in the river, all right, and the kids stopped swimming there and when they went to school knew if they saw it they would learn something not in the books. The Men's Up-to-Date Club rented a platoon of rowboats and rowed out to look. Something moved down deep in the water, and they hustled back to shore pronto. Winter came, and Spring came, and up it floated one day, and it <u>was</u> a sea serpent!..........For a while our town was called the deserted village. Says Grandpa Penny.

HALLOWEEN

"Why do we make pumpkin faces tonight?" Jeb asked.

"Up in Massachusetts long ago," Old Nat replied, "they had witches, boy. And one witch wanted awful bad to cross a bridge going into town. That witch's name was Goody Brink, and she had a cottage out in the piney woods. And she kept a mean-looking cat. Well, the townfolk, when they saw her coming, set up a regular army of men holding musket-guns. They didn't want Goody Brink to step into their town if they could help it. 'I could cross the river in an eggshell if I wanted to!' Goody cried, but they knew she was a liar. Even a witch, if she don't have a broomstick, has to cross a bridge by foot. 'Go home, Goody!' they yelled. 'This is one town you ain't getting into!' Now, they got tired of standing vigil, so somebody got the idea to carve some pumpkin heads, see, sticking candles inside so's she could see them in the dark. Then the townfolk all marched home and got forty winks. When Goody came next to the bridge, she stood there shaking her fist, cursing them pumpkins out. She declared, 'What's the matter? Ain't you good enough to speak to me?' She stood there and grew so mad she turned into a mud puddle!"

Suddenly Old Nat and Jeb heard a rustling in the bushes and a long low kind of moan. Maybe it was Goody and maybe it wasn't. They didn't wait to find out. They ran away as fast as their feet could carry them if not faster. Only the pumpkins know — but they're not telling.

DON'T SMOKE

Mrs. Thornberry was a widow, and her place was a good one to hang around, because she had a daughter down in Florida and was often visiting. The delicious sour crabapples at the side porch tree were there for picking, and you could climb up on the low roof on the kitchen and proceed carefully scrunching up the entire shingled roof to the peak and gaze out over the whole county and shout, "HALLOOOOOOO!"

One day, Oscar and Fergus Groll thought about fishing and they thought about chasing the fat Fortunato sisters, but they decided it was time to start smoking instead. With two corncob pipes, some cornsilk and stick matches, they settled themselves down behind Mrs. Thornberry's and got to work. "Shoo, Tipp!" they shooed, but Tipp wouldn't be shooed. Oscar lit one, and Fergus lit one, and they watched the red glow starting inside the corncob bowls.

"This is the life!" said Oscar.

"This is terrific!" added Fergus.

"No it isn't," said Oscar.

"You're not kidding," said Fergus.

"I feel sick," said Oscar.

"Sick as a dog," said Fergus.

But Tipp wasn't sick.

"Sick as a dog, my paw!" said Tipp to himself. "Sick as a boy who smokes corncob pipes, I'd say!"

THE BIG GAME

Eddie McNutt was the team's official runt. If the team had only been larger he would have been water boy. He didn't look like much in his helmet, cleats, and pads, you had to admit. However he had dreams of making his touchdown before the season's close.

It was the big game of the year, tied 0 to 0 at the end of the last quarter. With thirty seconds yet to play. The cheerleaders, the Sprenger sisters, Mavis and Edna, were going crazy there on the edge of Willhoff's cornfield.

Back in the huddle, Gaffer Dulong and Skinny Longnecker etched the play in the dirt with a stick while Little Eddie looked on feeling left out as usual. Once more the ball was hiked and it passed over heads and bounced in Little Eddie's direction. There was a mad scramble! Fingers flying! Bodies twisting—all for that wild, wild ball! It scooted in and out of grabbing arms, bounded between bony knees! When all the pouncing stopped and the dust cleared, there was Little Eddie racing with the ball. Toward the end zone.

Everybody and his brother piled on Little Eddie. "Get the runt!" grumbled everybody.

Then Bang!

PoP sssssssss!

"I'm shot!" cried Eddie.

He wasn't but the football was. Eddie had made his touchdown. And the game was over just in time.

5,001

Amos Grundy and Sam Spangler had been playing checkers together for about twenty-five years. They kept their score of wins and losses carefully on yellow lined paper. You might call it sort of a lifetime checker tournament. Sam was leading, 5,000 games to 0. He liked it that way because he liked to win. Amos kept trying and his motto was Don't give up. You can't lose them all.

Now Game 5,001 began pretty much like any other game. Sam and Amos sat in their regular chairs—Sam looking confident and unbeatable—Amos nervously rubbing his white rabbit's foot. Rain was banging loudly on the windows and there was the rumble of thunder shaking overhead.

Sam was playing the blacks. Amos was playing the reds. Neither man spoke. Sam moved. Amos moved. Sam moved. Amos moved. But Amos for once was making all the right moves.

He double-jumped Sam.

And triple-jumped Sam.

He made one king and another king.

Amos played the game of his life and he won it!

"Rats!" said Sam. He wasn't used to losing; after winning 5,000 straight games a loss was pretty hard to take. He grumbled, "But I'm still 4,999 games ahead of you, Amos."

"Maybe so," said Amos, "but we got 5,000 games to go. I'm going to <u>win</u> this tournament!"

SNOWMAN

Tom Pringle had formed the snowman in the likeness of Grandpa Penny himself. Tom thought he had gotten it down pretty accurately, because the old fellow never ventured out without his pipe, his moustache, and his scarf. Grandpa Penny looked funny enough, but Tom thought the snowman looked even funnier and was admiring his handiwork.

Then who but Grandpa Penny should come whistling down the street! Grandpa's mind was on eggs; he had been thinking about an omelet for lunch. And suddenly he saw this snowman standing where none had been standing before.

"Well sir!" said Grandpa Penny. "Ain't you new in town?" He stopped in his tracks. He leaned first on one foot, then another.

Then model and subject were standing face to face. Rather than stick around, Tom hid in back of the snowman. Grandpa Penny circled around the piece of sculpture to view it from all sides, and Tom had to keep circling too, to keep hiding from Grandpa Penny.

"Haw Haw!" laughed Grandpa Penny. Tom couldn't believe his ears.

"If that ain't the funniest snowman I've ever seen! It's the spitting image of Uncle Max!"

Tom sighed with relief. He'd forgotten Grandpa Penny couldn't see a thing without his bifocals.

THE ADVENTURERS

The thermometer said near to zero yet nothing could stop Redbeard (Fergus Groll) or Wolf Tooth (his brother Oscar) from braving the outdoors. It was a bone-chilling day.

They stuffed saltines in their pockets and set out heading for the lost country of Ukka Tukkatuk, through the frozen Arctic tundra (which led from one snowy yard into another). Their faithful husky, Tipp, followed.

"Is that the great polar bear I spy?" questioned Redbeard. It was Mrs. Girty's cat, Feathers, prowling under icicle-hanging bushes. The wind whistled through the trees.

Their teeth chattered and their bodies trembled till Wolf Tooth and Redbeard remembered they could be taking the warm bath their mother, Mrs. Groll, had told them to take. The search for Ukka Tukkatuk was abandoned! They trotted home and into the tub they jumped, the fierce Redbeard and the hearty Wolf Tooth, into the steamy water, to get thawed out. "Do Arctic explorers take baths?" asked Redbeard.

"Not more than once a year," said Wolf Tooth. "Cut it out, Tipp!" he yelled. Tipp helped—with his sandpaper tongue.

"Shouldn't we think about looking for a warm lost counry? Did you hear about El Kishmoor, and the fair Arab princess Coo Coo Cheh?" suggested Redbeard. "It's across this wild fantastic desert to the south..." His brother, Wolf Tooth, was listening. Already he could feel the hot stinging sand....

BASKETBALL

Skinny Longnecker, Chimp Gluss, Jr., Babe Minick, and Noodle Hennessey played basketball nightly in the school gym, but every game seemed to find them having an argument. About anything. Their voices would be raised in a chorus. It would go something like this, in case you could separate any of the words:

"You can't bang into me like that!"

"You chicken-livered grasshopper!"

"My basket was good, you guys!"

"Aw-w-w, only if cheating counts!"

"Oh yeah?" "Oh YEAH?"

That was the South End basketball group. Their coach, Stuff Bindle, warned them, but their voices continued to ring forth strongly, bouncing off the yellow tiled walls. You would hear:

"Why can't you play basketball as well as you open your mouth?"

"I keep getting the basketball and your head mixed up!"

"Oh, go back and sit in the gravel again!"

"Is that why they call you Four Eyes?"

"Oh yeah?" "Oh YEAH?"

Coach Bindle got fed up and said, "All right, you guys, no more basketball! Take a shower! Turn in your uniforms forever!" They did, but Skinny, Chimp, Babe, and Noodle still meet Thursdays upstairs in Miss Sook's room, 403. They call themselves the South End Debating Society.

QUICK-THINKING BEN

It was so cold the icicles were three feet long, the pump was frozen, and if it weren't for the dry gas and the horseblankets on the hood, the car wouldn't have started and Aunt Emmy wouldn't have kept her dental appointment with Doc Pingle, leaving Ben to watch the cookies she was baking in the oven and take them out soon enough. Ben wandered about the house while Aunt Emmy was gone; he enjoyed being in charge. When the telephone rang he answered it in a voice as deep and low as he could. "Mrs. Loose is not at home." He wrote his name at the windowpanes, then all the names he could think of. Next he wandered outside though it was cold as anything, playing tag with Ginger from the hen house to the stoop again, when he happened to glance up to the kitchen window—seeing smoke! Billowing out of the oven!

The cookies were burning!

He rushed to the pump. It was frozen. He breathlessly raced into the kitchen. The cookies were too hot to take out!

So he melted a bunch of snow in a pan.

Poured the panful of boiling water into the teakettle.

Poured the teakettle of boiling water over the frozen pump.

Pumped the pump till his muscles ached.

Rushed to the rescue with the cold water into the kitchen which by now was filled with black, rolling smoke.

And put out the sizzling cookies. Aunt Emmy drove up. "I got the pump working again," said quick-thinking Ben.

GRANDPA'S MAGIC SKATES

The snow is hardly finished flying, the pond hardly frozen over, before Grandpa Penny is out there honing his skate blades and fastening the ankle straps. A swig of hot black coffee and off he whizzes.

And if he thinks you are worth telling it to he will tell about the famous time when he skated all the way from one end of the Great Lakes across to the other. His name was in all the newspapers, he says. It was the hard winter of 1908. You should see him write out "1-9-0-8" on the ice! He started that marathon from the far western part, that would be Duluth, Minnesota, where he was visiting relatives (his brother Bink, wife, and child). The wind was behind him and the ice felt smooth and thick and away he raced down Lake Superior with a flock of crows following. That first night he pitched camp under the bright stars on Isle Royale along with a moose or two. Then up early in the morning, and soon he was skating nimbly through the Locks at Soo Saint Marie. Word was passed along and he was met with hot coffee, fried fish, and military bands; at Chicago, Illinois, on Lake Michigan, by the Mayor. Then on again. By this time folks were lined up along the lake shores to cheer him. At Cleveland, Ohio, they shot up fireworks and now he was whizzing bolder and bolder till suddenly he found himself skittering to the brink of Niagara Falls—there was nothing to do but leap! Lake Ontario at last!

It's all down there in the newspapers, Grandpa says.

THE GOLDEN COMET

Dad (Earl) De Witt saw the Golden Comet sled standing there shining in Hinkle's Hardware Store window; it was just like the Golden Comet he had owned when he was a boy. So he went in to buy it for his son, Earl Junior.

"That will be nine dollars," said Mr. Hinkle himself, taking it out of the window. Dad paid the money, carrying it out of the store eager as everything.

He took it home, then father and son, with the Golden Comet in tow, climbed to the top of Shoop Hill, which was great for sledding once you got to the top.

"Hop on, Junior. I'll show you how we did it in the old days!" said Dad. He was pretty excited. "Hold tight!" he instructed.

Well, down the hill they zoomed, lickety split. The other sledders watched, astonished. "There is nothing like a Golden Comet!" cried Dad, and he was right. ZOOM!

First Dad fell off, then Junior fell off. But the Golden Comet just kept on going, the snow was that good, all packed and slicked for sledding. Z O O M !

Dad and Junior chased the sled, but it was faster than they were. Down the hill it went! Right into town! Straight down Main Street! And CRASH! Back into Hinkle's Hardware Store window!

"That'll be fifteen dollars," said Mr. Hinkle.

TRIO

Everybody thought Amos Grundy and Sam Spangler were a little odd, not to say unmusical, because whenever they practiced together Zero howled right alongside and they didn't do anything about it. Which was okay for dog lovers but pretty hard on music lovers.

After a strenuous bit of tuning up on Amos's cello and Sam's clarinet they would get going, jumping immediately into a piece like "Magnolia at Eventide" or a snappy march such as "Pride and Joy." Zero would come racing from the kitchen!

The clarinet would tootle and the cello would saw away—and somewhere between the high notes of the one and the low notes of the other Zero would join in, and while he never sang it the same way twice, that was all right, because Amos and Sam believed in plenty of freedom of expression too.

Nobody dropped by when they practiced, which was Wednesday night. Windows were shut tight up and down the street, and Mrs. Early thought about calling out the A.S.P.C.A.

They became the laughingstock of town, and if either Sam or Amos went up to the Wig-Wam Cafe or to Schaff's Drug Store he was teased, pestered, or ridiculed.

Well—the town is laughing out of the other side of its mouth! The trio is now called Man's Best Friends, and they're the new sound sensation on coast-to-coast TV. You can catch them on the Sunday Amateur Hour.

DOG FOR SALE

Jared bought a dog.

He called the dog Charlie.

Charlie loved a lot of things, including yellow cheese, ginger snaps, and new shoes. Charlie also loved to sleep in Jared's bed. In fact, whenever you saw Jared you were bound to see Charlie; they followed each other everywhere.

When the ground was still frozen, the skunk cabbage, the first flower of the year, bloomed.

Jared showed it to Charlie. Charlie loved the skunk cabbage.

Charlie loved, too, to go visiting. The town dump, the red squirrels in the woods, the school yard, the firehouse, Crowe's Bakery, Shoop's Hill. Then when Spring was over and Summer had arrived Charlie suddenly got tired of visiting and just lay around, and Jared grew worried.

"I think Charlie has spring fever a little late in the season," decided Jared.

Charlie would not budge an inch, just lying in patches of sunlight, soaking up the sun.

"Charlie, get up!" Charlie <u>wouldn't</u>.

Jared tried giving Charlie vinegar mixed with molasses. Which, it turned out, Charlie did not love.

Charlie just lay there and grew fatter and fatter. Charlie slept and snored. "Charlie cannot be going to the icebox," reasoned Jared. Charlie grew fatter and fatter yet, and lazier and sleepier.

"This is the worst case of spring fever I have ever heard of," said Jared. "Charlie—what is the matter?"

Charlie should have been named Arlene.

THE END